Where's Julius?

JOHN BURNINGHAM

JONATHAN CAPE
Thirty-Two Bedford Square London

Among other books by John Burningham

Borka (Winner of the 1964 Kate Greenaway Award)
ABC
Seasons
Mr Gumpy's Outing (Winner of the 1971 Kate Greenaway Award)
Mr Gumpy's Motor Car
Around the World in Eighty Days
Come Away from the Water, Shirley
Time to Get Out of the Bath, Shirley
Would You Rather . . .
The Shopping Basket
Avocado Baby
Granpa (Winner of the 1984 Kurt Maschler Emil Award)

First published 1986
Copyright © 1986 by John Burningham
Jonathan Cape Ltd, 32 Bedford Square, London WC1B 3EL

British Library Cataloguing in Publication Data

Burningham, John
  Where's Julius?
  1. Title
  823'. 914 [J]   P27
  ISBN 0-224-02411-6

Printed in Italy by New Interlitho SpA, Milan

"For breakfast," said Mrs Troutbeck, "we have scrambled eggs with mushrooms, cornflakes and some orange juice, which I have unfrozen.

Where's Julius?"

Mr Troutbeck called their son Julius and they all sat down to breakfast.

"For lunch today we are having sardines on toast, a roll and butter, tomatoes, and nothing for pudding.

Where's Julius?"

"Julius says he cannot have lunch with us today because he has made a little home in the other room with three chairs, the old curtains and the broom."

So Mr Troutbeck took the tray with the sardines on toast, a roll and butter, tomato and no pudding to the other room where Julius had made his little home out of three chairs, the old curtains and the broom.

"I've got the lamb casserole for supper out of the oven and the potatoes in their jackets and broccoli with butter on top and for afterwards there is roly-poly pudding.

Where's Julius?"

"Julius says he cannot have supper with us just at the moment because he is digging a hole in order to get to the other side of the world."

So Mrs Troutbeck took the lamb casserole, the potatoes in their jackets and broccoli with butter on top and the roly-poly pudding for afterwards to where Julius was digging his hole.

"For breakfast there is sausage, bacon and egg, toast and marmalade and also a glass of Three-Flavour Fruit Juice.

Where's Julius?"

"Julius says he cannot have breakfast with us today because he is riding a camel to the top of the tomb of Neffatuteum which is a pyramid near the Nile in Egypt."

So Mr Troutbeck took the tray with the sausage, bacon and egg, toast and marmalade and the glass of Three-Flavour Fruit Juice – and another for the camel – to Egypt where Julius was riding to the top of the pyramid.

"For lunch there is cheese salad with celery and tomato and an orange for pudding if you want it.

Where's Julius?"

"Julius says he cannot have lunch with us just at the moment because he is cooling the hippopotamuses in the Lombo Bombo River in Central Africa, with buckets of muddy water."

So Mr Troutbeck took the tray with the cheese salad with celery and tomato and the orange for pudding to Africa where Julius was pouring buckets of muddy water on the hippopotamuses, to keep them cool.

"Here are the grilled chops for supper. There are baby carrots, garden peas and mashed potato to go with them, and an apple crumble for pudding.

Where's Julius?"

"Julius says he can't have supper with us just at the moment because he is throwing snowballs at the wolves from a sledge in which he is crossing the frozen wastes of Novosti Krosky which lies somewhere in Russia where the winters are long."

So Mrs Troutbeck took the tray with the chop, the baby carrots, garden peas and mashed potato and the apple crumble for pudding to Novosti Krosky which lies somewhere in Russia whcrc Julius was throwing snowballs at the wolves.

"For breakfast we are having boiled eggs, toast and marmalade and the Tropical Fruit Juice that you wanted.

Where's Julius?"

"Julius says he cannot have breakfast with us just at the moment because he is watching the sunrise from the top of the Changa Benang mountains somewhere near Tibet."

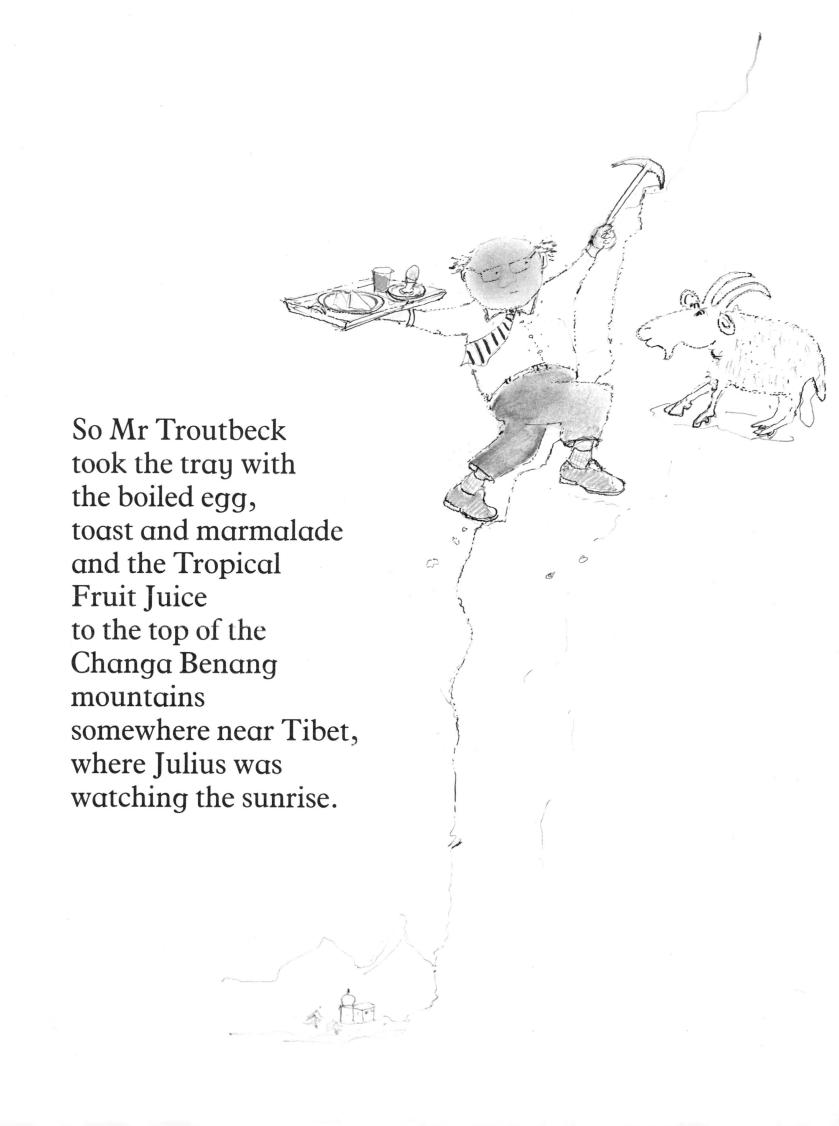

So Mr Troutbeck
took the tray with
the boiled egg,
toast and marmalade
and the Tropical
Fruit Juice
to the top of the
Changa Benang
mountains
somewhere near Tibet,
where Julius was
watching the sunrise.

"For lunch we are having spaghetti bolognese with lettuce and cucumber. For pudding there is plum duff.

Where's Julius?"

"Julius says he can't have lunch with us at the moment because he is on a raft which he has made from pieces of wood and old oil drums and he is about to shoot the rapids on the Chico Neeko River somewhere in Peru in South America."

So Mrs Troutbeck took the tray with the spaghetti bolognese, the lettuce and cucumber and the plum duff to the Chico Neeko River in South America where Julius was about to shoot the rapids on his raft.

"For supper today there is Lancashire hot-pot,
and steamed pudding for afterwards.

Is Julius building a home out of old curtains,
chairs and the broom?

Digging a hole to get to the other side of the world?

Riding a camel up a pyramid?

Cooling the hippos that stand in the
Lombo Bombo River?

Throwing snowballs at wolves in Novosti Krosky
where the winters are long?

Is he climbing the Changa Benang mountains,
or shooting the rapids on the Chico Neeko River
in South America?

Perhaps he is helping the young owls to learn
to fly in the trees at the end of the road
or tucking the polar bears in their beds
somewhere in Antarctica?"

"Betty," said Mr Troutbeck, "tonight Julius is having supper at home."